Keep It Inside

and Other Weird Tales

Mark Anthony Smith

For Tommy Andrew Skelton, who wanted to be Jason Vorhees but sang instead

About the Author

Mark Anthony Smith was born in Hull. His writings have appeared in many of The Small Press including 'The Horror Tree: Trembling with Fear', 'Fiction Kitchen Berlin', 'The Cabinet of Heed' and 'Penumbric Speculative Fiction Magazine'. Many of his Horrors have also surfaced in Anthologies. *Hearts of the Matter* and *Something Said* are available on Amazon.

Facebook: Mark Anthony Smith – Author
Twitter: MarkAnthonySm16

3

Contents

Artist @GunnarLarsenArt

The Prairie Lures

I don't know if I can go through it again. Even in the cold light of day my palms are sweaty. It was supposed to be the trip of a lifetime. Gosh! I remember being told I was going to Canada. I was asleep in the wagon at the time. I nearly bloody fell out the door when the Staff Sergeant told me. I thought I'd get charged for kipping. But he just laughed as I lunged forward and he said, 'Driver Phelps. Pack your kit. You're going to Canada for three months.' My parents were thrilled, of course. Most of the other lads were off to fight in The Gulf.

I was serving in 'The Royal Corps of Transport.' Our job in Alberta was to support the Tanks on Exercise and drain Medicine Hat of alcohol. We soon got used to cross country driving down the slippery Rattlesnake Road at British Army Training Unit Suffield or BATUS for short. I never got used to the sub-zero temperatures though. It was bitterly cold on the Prairie. You had to wrap up at night.

I went out to support some Infantry lads on Patrol. It started with a kick as I was woken up from a deep sleep. "It's your stag, mate." I swore. It was 2am and I had to get out of my sleeping bag to sit in a trench for two hours. I took a deep breath, counted to ten, and faced the biting winds. The lad was pleased to be relieved of his duty. I begrudgingly took his place as he muttered 'thanks' and I grunted. My rifle was freezing cold and I had to wake up, as

I leaned against the parapet, keeping an eye open for enemy patrols. I lit a cigarette and cupped it so the cherry wasn't visible to anyone that might have been doing a Reconnaissance. I really couldn't be arsed at that time of night.

There was a cluster of trees, to my right, and flat open ground elsewhere. I felt so pissed off and tired. It was cloudy. My night vision started to improve as I stubbed my cig out. Then, I noticed lights in the trees. I straightened up. They swam about like Will o' the Wisps. I was mesmerized. Then I looked at my watch. The two hours guard duty had flown by. I was relieved at 4am.

I didn't think of the pleasant distraction in the trees for long as I shivered in my sleeping bag. I soon warmed up and sleep took over. I was later shaken again. The usual rude awakening. I counted to ten and unzipped my bed to face the cold morning. I had a quick strip-wash that nipped my testicles and the I shaved, before eating porridge from my mess tin.

The day was spent cross country driving and servicing the Tank Targets. I fed the gophers some brown biscuits and night fell. I was called upon to join a Reconnaissance Patrol. There were reports of enemy in the woods.

We set out to see how many there were and what sort of kit they had. We might have needed to call in the Artillery or an Air strike if they had field guns. Our job was to stay out of trouble and not be seen. We just had to report our observations. Me and five other lads set out on Patrol. But only I came back. I can still see the fucking entrails...

There was no light as we entered the forest. We had to ghost walk through the trees as there were twigs underfoot and it was prime trip wire territory. The sky was cloudy again. We took our time so as not to alert anyone. The roosting birds in the trees were calling to each other. I found this unusually eerie. We were cautious. Then, a muffled scream. I dropped to the ground. There was confusion. I waited. "Someone has snatched the tail-end Charlie." *Oh, for fuck's sake,* I thought. We had to find the last man in our patrol. But we didn't. We re-grouped. There were arguments and lads lashing out. "Let's go back!" "Let's carry on!" "Oh, for fuck's sake."

We decided to abort the Recce and return to base. The missing man would be at our last rendezvous, we thought. But he wasn't. And the trees were closing in. We quickened our pace as what little humour we had left turned to fear. This wasn't a daft joke after all. There was something amiss. I thought there were shadows in the trees. We hurried. The shadows were real. And then I felt suddenly alone. I was cut off from the patrol.

I won't lie. I was absolutely shitting myself. What the hell were those lights last night? They'd been strangely calming. But now the forest was a living hell. I was lost and disorientated. I stopped to find my bearings. Then I saw the bastards. They must have been nearly ten feet tall. They weren't

Sasquatches, but they walked like men. I will never forget those dark red eyes. It was like looking into a blood bath. I screamed, "Help!" Any notion of being tactical had passed. I was fighting to stay alive. I must have hit every single branch as I ran. I dropped my kit. Then I threw up. There were steaming innards hanging off a branch like perverse Christmas tinsel. It was a complete mockery. I threw up again. Then I ran. I ran all the way back and passed out.

On my return to Colchester, there were rumours. None of the lads had come back off the patrol. "You'll be seeing The Commanding Officer for manslaughter," some of the lads said. "Fuck off!" I snorted. I was confused. I needed peace and quiet. Whatever those things were, they weren't wolves or escaped animals from the zoo. I think they were something more. I mean, they were nearly ten foot tall.

I will never recover from my Canadian trip. It was supposed to be a once in a lifetime blessing. But I lost some good mates to those cannibalistic savages. I'm hoping to get a job on Civvy Street now. But until then, I try to stomach a few books on Indian Folklore. It's too much.

Wood Fooks

"It was definitely your idea to stay at this dump!" Nigel doesn't reply. He's too busy looking through the grimy windowpane that he'd just put through with the pitchfork. I wish we had never come here. The Farmer who we rented the barn conversion off, for the weekend, looked really dodgy. Each eye of his was in conflict with the other. Maybe, one of them was lazy. He'd warned us about the kids.

They weren't really teenagers though. They were grown men running through the trees. They had rifles too. I didn't know why. Last night, they were trespassing here. Making stupid noises and drinking ale from bottles. I think they were looking for the Wood Fooks. Maybe, they were the Wood Fooks themselves. It was hard to tell. I know strange creatures are being researched at East Yorkshire University. But me and Nigel put it down to an old wives' tale. We just wanted to rent this gaffe, near Goadley, so we could fish over the weekend. It's dark now.

"They're definitely back," stammers Nigel. I am careful. There's broken glass everywhere. I can't believe he reacted like a film hero. "Can you see anyone?"

The trees are closing in. The shadows and the dark make me more alert and claustrophobic. The odd bird calls its warning sign. Then it's quiet. I listen to Nigel's breathing. He falls back from the sill. "What the fuck was that?" He is panicking.

I look out. It's quiet on the mud clearing where the bent Farmer parks his Land Rover. There are shadows. I can see my breath. Then it comes out. It's dragging one of the men. He looks quite dead as the thing pulls him along. I imagine a trail of blood. The thing has cloven feet like a goat and long hair where its neck should have been. It's snorting and bellowing through its snout. Those fucking eyes! I can't look.

"Come here, my pretty!" The bloody farmer is greeting it. "What have you brought me?" I can see there's a leg missing now that the farmer has a torch. I can feel my heart. The beast lets go of its prey. It screams louder. It's like a screech. Then the farmer struggles. He drops to the ground. "Fuck, Nigel. Fuck! We've got to go." Nigel is gibbering something about dying. I wait for the ape-goat to pick up the corpse, or what is left of it. It lurches back into the trees.

I start. I dash out to the farmer, but he is quite dead. He is almost unrecognizable as his insides are steaming in the cold. There is nothing I can do for him. I feel nauseous at the pool of abattoir. I feel my legs shaking. Then I climb inside the farmer to disguise myself. The carnage is warm and sticky. I pull his skull over my head.

Nigel screams. I dash back in my second skin. I am too late. The Wood Fook is tearing at his arm. It smells of dead pilchards amongst the copper smell of blood. Nigel has stopped pleading. I gulp for air.

"There, my pretty. What have you brought me?" It lurches round with its red mottled eyes. Its sinewy pelt is matted with my friend. It bares its crappy teeth as it looks down on me. I'm thinking I've bitten off more than I can chew. These things aren't that stupid. I can feel my bowels loosen. The thing is eyeing me up. It bares its teeth.

Then it offers the best of Nigel. I want to throw up. My head is spinning. I know I couldn't outrun this monster. Several more are coming out of the night. They have been lured by the smell of spilt blood. I can't run for it. I take part of my friend.

It was a really bad idea coming to this ruined farmhouse. We sensed this in the car. The roads were quiet. We saw how isolated this place is. Nigel was so excited. He talked about gutting trout and eating it with instant mashed potatoes cooked on our portable stove. He gestured how big some of the fish were with his arms outstretched. I almost laugh with panic now. Nigel's arm is dismembered. What will I tell his parents?

I nod. I bite into my childhood friend and think of sushi. I chew as I try to look appreciative. My children gather and feast. It seems that I've managed to outwit them. I tear at Nigel's flesh to save my life. I think he would want that now. I chew and think of sushi. Then I realise this meat is not so bad. I bite again. I rip at him with hunger. The beasts are feeding too.

Then a claw reaches for my face. I pull back but it squeezes the farmer's chin until his head falls back. My face is covered in a clammy death. The thing rises. It towers above me as I scramble to my feet. The skin falls from me like a grizzly overcoat. I need to think fast. I can see Nigel's pitchfork. I drop to my knees again and scramble. One of the ape-goats beats me to it. I scream as the prongs embed in my stomach. I try to pull away. The thing lunges the fork at me again with its primitive claws.

I fall beside what is left of the farmer and my friend. These things are hungry for flesh. I think about displacing myself. I'm past thinking about fish. I start to pray with a newfound faith. I'm not sure what to ask for anymore. I feel a claw inside my belly. It pulls as I feel something tear and give. I am losing consciousness. The light is dimming as the beasts turn to me. I am trying to think of somewhere else as my bones are stripped. I feel naked and exposed to a night that will always be black. It will be dark. I feel cold. I am naked. I hope I see Nigel again.

The Clifftop Terrors

Dave really hates caravan holidays. But Holly, his wife, tells him to think about the children. Dave think about James and Carl. They're laughing in the rear-view mirror. He keeps his eyes on the small, winding road. There are thick clouds which makes the day feel later than it is. Dave hopes it's not going to rain all week. It's bad enough when it's sunny on the resort. He thinks about a barbeque with choice steaks and a cold beer. It's not all bad once you get used to slumming it.

Dave hated exercises, even with The Rifles. They were out every three weeks or so. He still can't believe he managed three years in The Infantry. He was a lot younger then. He didn't question much, and he aimed to please. The rations were awful, and it always chucked it down when they were digging in. Sleeping in a trench was the pits. There'd always be tree roots where they had to clear the earth. Dave smiled to himself. The holiday camp was marginally better, but he'd need a proper holiday to get over this week.

The family pass by the village green in Goadley. It is a quiet place with a 16th century church and one shop that is also a Post Office. They'd been to this part of East Yorkshire before. The coastal road is quiet. There are fields everywhere with the odd smatterings of wooded areas on the rural horizon. They can see the wind turbines, in the distance, that sit out on The North Sea at the seaside resort a way up the coast. This area of the coastline is eroding faster than the national average. Huge slabs of chalk cliffs are being eaten by the tides.

Dave is thinking about tonight's kids' entertainment and the annoying bear with the clichéd jokes that have probably been butchered from last season. Some of those characters are really creepy. You never know who is dressed up in their cosplay. They'll have been Police-checked, he supposes. So, that's reassuring. It must be hot in those suits though. Dave feels hot under the collar himself. He pulls his jumper and t-shirt from his neck. It feels tight and restricted. As he lets go, Holly grabs his arm tight. Dave jumps.

"I've just seen something," she quakes. Dave notices the unease in her tenor. He brushes it off.

"It was probably a deer," Dave replies. "Boys? Did you see anything?" The kids absently say, "No." They are excited about the amusements and the pedal boats at the park. Holly is quiet.

"It was much bigger than a deer," she breathes. "It was... They were much bigger."

"What do you mean?" Dave asks. She thinks for a moment. Holly is trying to process something.

"They walked between two and four legs. One of them looked me straight in the eyes," she shudders.

"Well, there aren't any bears around here," Dave states. "Except for the comedy one." Holly doesn't respond. She is looking at somewhere that doesn't exist. "I'm sorry," he says. "I didn't mean to fob you off." Holly forces a smile.

"It was probably nothing," she brushes, but Dave can see she's perturbed.

"We're nearly there now. Is it too early for check-in?" Holly moves the box of tissues from the dashboard clock.

"Nope! It's all going to plan." The boys ask their Mother questions as Dave concentrates on the last leg. The road is narrow along these parts. It starts spitting with rain. Dave isn't sure why Holly is so jumpy these days.

They pull up to the resort. A sign reads 'closed.' The gate is shut too.

"What the heck?" Holly opens the door and tries the intercom. It's quiet. She shrugs her shoulders.

"Try it again," Dave mouths. She presses it again, but her husband can't hear the reply. The gate mechanically opens as Holly gets back in the car.

"It's just a glitch, apparently." They had expected it to be really busy at this time of day. The car park across from the reception is packed but they eventually find a parking space after braking for a few kids. "They need to watch where they're going," Dave mutters. A young blonde-haired boy flicks up two fingers and his Mum laughs. Holly is incredulous. Dave turns the engine off.

"Have you got the booking form?" Holly gives Dave some papers and he heads over to check-in. There's a large queue. He taps his feet and thinks about a Spanish beach somewhere. There're excited kids everywhere here. So, it's hard to escape with his thoughts. Eventually, he reaches the albino-looking receptionist. "Why was the gate locked?" She looks up from the form.

"Just a few glitches, Sir. Everything is fine!" Dave thinks, actually, that he doesn't think it's fine. He wonders who she is trying to reassure. She gives him the caravan keys and a map which she has circled. They're furthest away from the amusements. It should be nice and quiet. Holly reads the plan.

"I don't know why they can't set these pitches out logically. It's like they've designed it as they've gone along. If design is the right word!" Holly nods. They drive around twice. Dave tries to stay calm. He can't understand why the gate was locked. They finally pull up to the 8-berth static.

"Home, sweet home!" he announces. Holly chuckles.

"It looks beautiful," she smiles. Dave fumbles at the door lock. It seems jammed. Then he notices someone has been trying to block the lock with chewing gum.

"They could have done a better job," he laughs, as he finally opens the door. "Well, it looks clean, but it smells of urine." Holly wrinkles her nose as the boys dash round.

"Yes. It does smell of piss," she agrees. Dave grabs some bags from the boot of the car and dumps them in the biggest bedroom. He opens the flat-pack wardrobe. There's a glossy. The pictures in the magazine makes his stomach churn. There're people tied up and some of them are in pain. He takes it out to the bin and dumps it.

***

Trevor Mason is fed up with playing Belinda the Bear. He's waiting to hear about train driver training which he applied for two months ago. Apart from seasonal farm work, there aren't many job opportunities in Goadley. He has to sit this season out again as a main character in the holiday kids' show. He's totally stressed out all the time. But arsing about in a bear suit pays the bills. He fumbles with the head and looks through the grinning mouth. Julie, who plays Egbert the Elephant, helps him into his pink tutu. She checks his matching headband is straight.

"Go get them, tiger," she laughs.

Trevor's stomach is rumbling. He mimes to a sound system recording and nods and shakes his head in the right places. Trevor is eyeing up the audience. There's a young woman in denim shorts with her daughter. He frolicks with Egbert through 'Jack and the Beanstalk.' The children laugh, "he's behind you!" Then they sound out the 'Goodbye Song' like cheerleaders. "Gee, Oh, Oh, Dee ..." every bloody night. He's glad when he can get out of his mincing hot suit. Belinda the Bear haunts his fucking dreams.

His acquired taste began as benevolence. Indeed, his stomach turned watching a true-life flick about the infamous *Slasher Jenkins*. How could the repulsed, young Trevor ever know that he'd become a copycat? It started out for the good of mankind; an almost philosophical 'tragedy of the commons' reasoning. There were things far worse. They were locking the campers in for crying out loud. Trevor wanted to stop the holiday makers coming. He had wanted to end the nightmares that were happening at the time. Since then, he has acquired a taste. He is surprised that the hundreds of missing punters haven't aroused suspicions. But it is still early in the season and Trevor has the taste of flesh on his tongue.

He wriggles out of the ridiculous Bear outfit and heads to the laundrette, with a hold-all, where it's quiet. It's blustery as the leaves rattle where he crouches in wait. The woman in the shorts always passes the laundrette after the children's show and the hour-long disco afterwards. The hunger is gnawing like a rodent. Trevor conjures up the sweet flesh as he pulls something heavy from the bag. He hears an excited child. It's the girl. Then Trevor screams. His leg is ripped from its socket as it's thrown across the Mother's path. Whatever mauled Trevor is feasting on his torn-up torso.

***

Holly and Dave have already been ripped apart near the swimming pool. The couple didn't stand a chance. Their sons are cowering near the amenities hut, paralysed with fear. They watch as the things pass by. The creatures came from the caves that pepper the cliffs. The wasted deer-like bodies support the resemblance of a human head. The creatures don't have necks and look awkward on their stilt-legs. Their high-pitched squeals and guttural groans echo anguish on the winds. They feast on human flesh.

The boys watch a herd of the blind deer-men pass on their skinny pins. James has an accident in his trousers.

"We have to leave," he shakes. Carl agrees. They make for the locked gate. There is carnage everywhere. No child should see this abattoir. The boys disappear, under the barrier and into the night back towards Goadley.

***

Trevor feels several nuzzles riving hungrily at his innards. The things evolved from the fossils in the cliffs where they will return. They blindly rip at Trevor's kidneys. The light of consciousness is dimming. Trevor prays that he will be forgiven for cooking up the flesh of campers. His is an odd methodology. He felt it was the lesser evil against these abominations. Trevor thinks about the pact that the proprietors have made. How can you reason with those beasts? Trevor prays as consumed prey. There are monsters of all sizes here and Belinda the Bear is hung up about that. His final breath expires. The creatures move on.

What the Trees Recall

Mother locks me in the spare room. Itch and scratch in here. My hair is matted on my arms and stomach. It feels like I've got lice. But my teeth are still sharp for tearing man's flesh. I haven't tasted it in a while. And I get convulsions from the withdrawals. I'm not bad. They say I am. I've heard them from the foot of the stairs.

My Mother says, "Nathaniel? You are the apple of my eye." I smile and nuzzle into her breast. I will do anything to win her favour.

The bare floorboards are damp, and the walls are peeling. There are draughts from the door and the smeared windows. I scrape my talons on the floorboards and comfort myself with Mother's words. I want to go outside again. Just once. But I mustn't upset the apple cart. I try to sing. My vocal cords are too primitive, so I listen to the trees.

The foliage in the breeze are as old as the moon and the tides. They murmur secrets. Bad secrets. I ask them what they know.

The trees know that we lived off the land. We lived amongst ourselves in peace. I don't remember that. It was before our litter was birthed. They know I'm not a bad apple too. They say I will feast again when the threat has gone. The threat of contamination. We used to live such simple lives. I ask the trees about my Father.

There are rumours amongst our folk that Mother slit his throat and hung him from the apple tree. But I don't think there's a grain of truth in that. And Mother has pipped the neighbours to the post. She said he was sent away for bringing something back. Something impure that would contaminate us. The trees are silent.

The trees tell me again from the beginning. It scares me, this story. Yet there's some comfort in it. They tell me that in the beginning there was a sow and a hog. They were happy together and ate any fruits in the forest. The world was their oyster.

The Great Forest King said, "All these trees I give you. But you must never eat from the apple tree." The sow and the hog praised the Great King.

Then man said to the sow, "The apples are good fruits. Why shouldn't you try one?" The sow tempted the hog. She sowed the seed. The hog succumbed to the delicious flesh. It tasted good. Then the Great Forest King banished the man. He cursed the sow and the hog to crave human flesh. That is why you live in enmity. That is why your community should be a walled community. Do not let anyone contaminate you.

We were happy in our stagnant pond. We didn't think too much and wanted for nothing. Then outsiders came. They brought the wheel and the crucifix. They talked about evolution and higher learnings. We didn't want progress. We wanted to live in peace. Some of the folk ventured out. They brought back human flesh riddled with diseases.

This created great unease. The rumours started to catch like wildfire. We talked less with our neighbours. Mother still talks with them now. But I must not go outside. She says it will harm my scales and my pelt will moult.

She tends the beautiful garden and talks with the neighbours. I watch her through the grime-encrusted pane as she swishes flies with her tail. I think about my Father. I don't remember much. There is nothing left of him in our house. All his things are gone. It is a blank slate except for the rotting shed that he built with his own four hands. I yearn to slip outside.

I itch and I peel and I pace the boards in soliloquy. I am my own company. The trees are my theatre. They remind me of how good the fruit tastes. The fruit of my Mother's labour. But I want meat. And I long to feel the breeze because the air in here is too close and musty. There is rage. Rage and impatience as I objectify my Mother. I forget about her tenderness and her unique affection. She holds me prisoner. I want to... I want to...

Remember the fruit, the branches whistle. We'll rustle up a fruit salad. I look to the trees. "Fuck the trees!" I am more than an Actor. I have very real yearnings. Yearnings and hungers that demand an audience bigger than one.

"The fruit! Your Mother's love." I don't want to feel, I want to think. I think. And then I think I know. There is a light in the growing darkness. It is time to find myself.

I feel the pang of fear. What if I melt or burn? It's a lie! You won't burn. No! But I'll blister real big. That's what happens to the bad apples who shake the apple cart. It's a lie! No. It is not. I realise this is self-doubt. I want to venture out and take away these uncertainties.

My mouth is dry. It doesn't remember the taste of anything good. I think about my Mother. Then I forget about her. I elbow the door. I barge until it splinters and breaks. I creep out but my toenails give me away. Then I chuckle as best as a simian reptile thing can. Why am I creeping? I have just disturbed the forest with my door-breaking rage. I feel emboldened. The forest listens to me. I hasten and lollop through the kitchen to the back door. There is the rusty key in the lock. But the door breaking is empowering. I smash the wood with a stumbled kick. My balance was never that good because my tail is still juvenile. I crash over the splinters and the spelks.

"Have some firewood to feed your rumours." I find this funny as I cross the path to my Father's shed. The door is weathered and unhinged. I peek into the gloom. Then I shrink or melt. There's something slumped in the corner. I cry out. Then Mother is here to take it all away.

Keep it inside

The wind rattles the old wooden peeling window frame as floorboards cool and contract. Kim listens to the lead pipes stutter and burp. Her Dad runs a bath. He shuts the bathroom door, muffling the running taps on the tin bath. Kim pulls her blankets up to her chin. She is used to noises at night since her Mother passed two years ago.

It was an awful accident and Kim wasn't allowed to identify the body with her Father. She was left outside and didn't know how to quell his tears. He has become a lot quieter since the loss. His comforting laugh is rare. The autumnal gusts disturb the old fireplace and there are scraping sounds. Kim pulls her bedclothes over her head. The floorboards creak as her Dad leaves the water to drain. She listens to wood on wood as her senses heighten.

Outside, an owl welcomes the night from a copse near Goadley. The Victorian house, with its huge back garden, is built in front of corn fields. Ian used to kick a ball and soak Kim with the hosepipe before he went through the windscreen. She misses her little brother. He had given her focus in her life as she teased and nurtured him. Now, she imagines that he is resting with Mam. The owl continues to pierce the dark. Later, it leaves her to the house.

It is quiet. Kim doesn't know what time it is. Downstairs, the television is barely audible, but she can just make out the theme to *Tales of the*

Unexpected. The stairs groan and the door pulls on carpet as her Dad peers in. She hears him retire and feels her heart against her chest. The wind is hammering on the wooden frames. It has picked up across the open fields. She listens to the tapping branches on the wooden fencing out the back. Tree shadows cast spectral fingers on fence lats. Then the Russian dolls start to dance on the mantlepiece again. That familiar hollow wood dragging on timber dragging sound.

Her parents had brought the wooden dolls back from their trip to Germany. Ian got a train with magnetic links that pulled the small lacquered carriages on etched timber tracks. She remembers how he set her dolls apart and gave the smallest one a ride on his engine. Kim used to hide marbles or an acorn in the halved dolls for Ian to guess where it was hidden. She'd try to catch him out with her magician's vanishing trick.

Kim can't stop thinking about Ian and Mam. She shudders at the thought of them hidden like the acorn that reappeared before wide eyes. Her pillow is damp. She brushes the gentle tears off her cheek. Her chest heaves. The dolls are dancing again. They scratch in the dark on the mantlepiece that Mam used to light with scrunched up newspapers on coals. It was cosy and reassuring then. The high bedroom ceilings eventually warmed as a soft voice read about talking woodland animals. She misses those stories before the final kiss. "Goodnight, Mam."

The scrapings cease. She thinks about why she was expelled from school. Kim is under Police investigation for gouging Bob Maddock's eyeball out like a stone amongst fleshy fruit. She clawed until the stalk ripped free. Everyone in the playground screamed or fainted as she held the gruesome trophy up in her bloodied fingers. Kim didn't anger easily, but their teasing was relentless. She had screamed, "Don't fuck with me." Then her hand released Bob's eye as she had a meltdown. The bike shed swam back into view and there was a breeze on her face again. Kim didn't know what had possessed her.

"I saw Ian running through the fields last night," said Martine, at school. Bob had said her brother is still alive. Other kids shared similar narratives too. It really made Kim's blood run cold. She imagines her little brother frozen in the short seven years of his life. She tries to imagine his torment; his blonde matted hair blowing in the chilly open fields. He had been a mess as he was flung through her Mam's windscreen. That tiny, twisted body with the sweetest smile. Then she feels the torn eyeball on the back of her hand. The dolls dance again on the mantlepiece.

The grief counsellor suggested the healing process would take two years. "It is different though, from person to person, because people are different and experience life in unique ways." Kim wasn't sure the therapist had experienced loss. The six sessions certainly didn't help. Talking with Mam does. Her Mam makes the dolls dance. They don't talk about Ian. Kim spends time in the fields and has forgotten about her GCSEs at North Humberston Secondary School. She worries about her Dad.

After Bob's eye was removed in the playground, all sorts of people have vented their angers. Dad had a meltdown as a brick was thrown through the living room window. It reminded them both of the shattered windscreen and their twisted family losses. The two bodies were a mess. "How the hell do we move on?" Father and daughter both looked into space. Her Dad is really struggling. Kim hasn't told him about the dancing dolls or the worst of the rumours. He'd crack. She thinks his grief is too much for him to bare.

The scrapings start more furiously. The Russian dolls pack and unpack; they dance and dance. "It's OK, Mam. I'm sure Ian is OK." The mantlepiece calms. Then Kim has the urge to find her coat. She carefully unlocks the front door and slips down the side of the house. She struggles to pull herself over the fence. The moon is full, and she stands on the muddied perimeter of the tall corn field. The wind is silent as corn ears blow. It's unusually still in the full moonlight. Then she sees Ian. He is laughing as he plays with all the other dead children. Kim smiles. Death has restored his legs.

She watches them run and tag each other. Kim knows not to shout his name. Her chest and stomach quieten down and she thinks how serene death might be. Ian runs in the fields. She's quite sure she'll see him again. Then a thought occurs. Are the children watching over the house? She wonders if they would dislodge the eyeball of someone, bent on revenge. The sickening is replaced with a lightness. Kim takes a last look at the gambolling kids and heads back to bed.

It is cold in her bedroom. The dolls move slower. The scraping is more pronounced as if the dolls are mulling something over or waiting for an answer. Kim falls on her bed. She feels different. Maybe she feels lighter. She pulls the jacket around her ears. Then she covers herself in blankets. Before sleep, she remembers how small her Mam looked as she faded away. Sleep is almost upon Kim as she parts her legs. "Come, Mam. Wrap yourself up." The Russian dolls quieten. They stop. And moving herself into the foetal position, her Mam re-enters Kim in reverse childbirth.

Crown of Slugs

My brother often took things too far, like jokes or binge drinking, and conquering his fears was no exception. I keep him in a jar now with breathing holes punched in the metallic screw-top lid. I don't know how much longer Seth will live. He can't talk anymore. He just writes in a rudimentary scrawl.

We talked about our fears. Seth said that his vertigo doesn't impact on his life. So, he could live with his fear of heights. He doesn't believe in evolution. But he does think that life adapts to its changing environment in small ways. I now know this to be true. I just think 'small ways' is an understatement given what's happened. He said, "Petra. You can't go on fearing mice and spiders. You should immerse yourself, through therapy, to overcome your emotions." I did.

I talked about spiders and I described the small rodents. Then, I watched videos as I bit my nails. I listed the good points. They play a part in food chains. Then finally, after breaking the therapist's nose, I petted a mouse and let a tarantula edge its way up my arm. I felt so empowered. I booked a family holiday to Spain. I thought Seth would wobble at the thought of flying. But he said the clouds cushioned his fears as he couldn't really look down. He'll never fly again. He's changed since that flight that he said 'wasn't a problem'.

31

Seth took some elective modules in Cryptozoology, at East Yorkshire University, towards his Degree in Anthropology. I know that Coelacanths have since been discovered after they were long thought extinct. I really didn't believe in devils or The Loch Ness Monster though. Not then. Now, I think that anything is possible. I wouldn't be surprised if 'Area 51' housed aliens.

Seth was finally due to leave Hellen Salads after eight years. He managed to get a job at the Holiday camp near Goadley. But it got closed down. The Press said that there'd been a lot of murders there. Some of our neighbours talked about unnatural things. I'm sure they're just old wives' tales. People have nothing better to do than gossip. So, Seth had to reapply for his old job.

From a young age, my brother poured salt or boiling water in the garden. Mam used to go mad at the slug carcasses scattered everywhere. "Are you scared of them?"

He laughed. "No! I'm just repulsed. I hate the way they rear up and slowly explore." He told me about an incident where one of the factory lads had chucked one at him. The dirty big black slug clung from his fringe as Seth bent forward. He screamed and shook his head to shake it off. Then he gave the lad a good hiding.

I can imagine how the lad had found out though. I often caught Seth in a trance as he watched a slug on the patio. It was so bad that he couldn't touch Shaun Hutson's debut book cover or the sequel: *Breeding Ground.* We talked about immersion. I reminded him how I learned to remove house spiders by gradations. Seth was resolute. He could never go down that path. Then he talked about Stanislavsky.

I don't know much about Method Acting but Seth became infatuated. He read about its psychological effects and how it helped the practitioner to 'get into character'. It wasn't long before I found Seth on his stomach. He wanted a slug's perspective on the world. I said, "I think that you're taking this a bit too far."

Seth laughed with the clichéd, "There's method in the madness." He was on his belly again, propelling himself, like some bizarre gym exercise. Not long after, a lump became a growth on his belly. His arms and legs were losing muscle mass too. Entropy kicked in.

I remember us giggling at Cronenberg's *The Fly* and I've read Kafka's *The Metamorphosis.* I can't think about Samsa's fate now. I had asked Seth to give his ideas up. But he was determined. He used his arms and legs so little that he eventually lost them. The belly foot took over. His skin became more mottled and darker too. Eventually, his world became smaller as his single-minded attention focused on overcoming his revulsion. In short, he became that which he hated. Seth is a slug.

I suppose the irony is that I now stand transfixed as Seth did. His only means of communication was a slow scrawl of slimy broken

English. After the tears and the horror, I brought myself to let him out in the rain-drenched garden. I watched for blackbirds and hedgehogs as my brother felt his way about. I realised that he'd really changed, one day, as he ascended a tree. He'd quite forgotten his fear of heights. I soon forgot the time. I had to forget that this leopard slug was my brother as a mate found him.

The second slug had picked up Seth's trail. It nibbled and nipped his detritus covered tail. They pulsated forward to the nearest branch. I had to forget this was my brother having sex. But it was quite a wonder as the two slugs wrapped around each other, like a snail's helix, on their silvery thread. They danced mid-air for hours. Then, I watched a penis emerge from behind their heads. They each looked flowered like an exotic orchid. These too seemed to dance, as each slug penetrated the other. It was difficult and fascinating at the same time. I had mixed emotions as both penises tried to untangle. The mate then bit my brother's cock off and he became a girl. This act of apophallation happens a lot, I later discovered. It was quite a gruesome shock watching it. The slugs then dropped free-fall into the leaves below them. The amputation writhed like a chopped worm. It was very much still alive.

My brother became a lot more withdrawn after the castration. He wanted to be called Shoala. The name was traced repeatedly before she laid her eggs outside. Soon, I had more nieces and nephews than I could count; the hatchlings were too numerous. Shoala spent more time at the rim of her jar when it was too dry outside. I couldn't understand her anxieties. Then she took me to the same tree where her member was dismembered. It still writhed. I let Shoala write 'territorial' in her snake-like slime writing. I followed, my sister, the slug.

She oozed over to a discarded house brick at the foot of the tree. As she disappeared, I lifted the brick and almost dropped it in disgust. About the size of a toad, the small abomination was slightly more human than gastropod. It was a man-slug king. Around its sticky temple were my sister's children. They formed a dancing crown on the thing's head. It was trying to usurp my sister. She has her own patch.

The slug-thing reared its head. Shoala hung back. Then the abomination struggled. It writhed as something tightened around its neck. I wanted to look away. I was torn. I watched the grip tighten and the thing keeled over.

Shoala died soon afterwards. In death, she became my brother again. I took Seth's body to the Cryptozoology office and left the carcass to be examined. Professor Grimshaw assured me that he'd treat Seth's body with the upmost respect. I didn't tell him the whole story. Indeed, sometimes, I awake sweat sodden to feel the sensation of a penis constricting my neck.

The Call to Dust

There were always missing dogs foraging in my Grandfather's garden. That's how he met his wife. A young Beatrice had followed her nose to retrieve her Springer and she became Mrs. Cleaver that same year. Apparently, she understood him. But she had passed on long before I came into this world. I only knew Grandad Ron as a single man.

He was fit for his years, with a great sense of humour – a warmth; a concrete certainty amongst the ordered disarray of his Victorian house on Pendrill Street. I never saw him in any other settings. The house was almost an extension of the man himself. It was fusty throughout and the rooms were filled with old things. My Grandfather liked taxidermy and archaeology. I'm not sure that he learned very much about what he'd collected over the years. His collection was vast. There were glassy eyed owls, stoats and posturing badgers with teeth bared for a frozen eternity. Then he had coins and bronzed spear tips that he'd unearthed with his metal detector. And all the time, those stray dogs fought and growled in Grandad Ron's garden. I suppose he was used to it.

I asked, "Do you like pets, Grandad?"

He smiled. Then he casually itched his mole. "Only if I don't have to feed them." We laughed as he was cleaning up some old muddied coins.

My Grandfather had kind, brown eyes that had seen too much yet were still softened from his heart. We laughed about his brother; the mole on his cheek - and how it gave him intuitive advice. He'd press the dark growth between thumb and forefinger to form a mouth. It spoke with a terrible Scottish accent. "Can ye dig?" he squeezed, as he gave it a life.

Once, I'd stuck my stick through the garden, to ward off each stray dog. I enjoyed spending time with him. I'm surprised that I'd never got bitten as the packs of hounds were rabid. "Why do they come here, Grandad? It's like a congregation." But as often as I asked – and I asked a lot – there never was an explanation. At least not until I had to clear his house after his death, anyway. And what I am about to reveal is only one world-truth although many people can agree on the same thing. But no-one would refute that a coffee table is called a table. So, there are external realities common to all.

I had to do a house clearance. That's when the dreams started. In death, I came to know him better than I ever did when he was alive. As I cleared out Grandad Ron's belongings, I began to unearth some truly curious secrets that really should not see the light of day. There are things that should be buried forever. There are also things that are beyond use – even the charity shop would not take away the aged furnishings. I had to take the worn chairs and stained upholstery to the household tip. I knew it would be a fair-sized job, but I'd underestimated the entirety of his life's haul, it seemed.

My Grandfather had a vast library. There were yellowed paperbacks where he'd folded the pages to mark where he'd previously left off. I hated that. My books were pristine. It seems he never used a bookmark. I looked around at the sizeable and fairly ordered collection. Behind a dusty desk, with papers and cuttings from periodicals, I saw a row of black leather books. Some of them were embossed with ornate gold lettering.

I took one from the shelf and dusted the dirt from the top of the tome. It had been printed by The Miskatonic University. Where had I heard of that place of learning? I looked through the strange inscriptions and diagrams. I felt a shudder run through my bones. I slipped the book back and sat at my Grandfather's desk to steady myself, wondering what sort of man he had been.

There are modern psychological arguments that suggest you become what you read or who you spend your time with. For instance, does a steady course of Horror Films make the viewer more desensitized to violence? I didn't think it did. And yet if a dressmaker repeats a posture for hours, over the course of a working lifetime, does he or she start to adopt shoulders that lean forwards? It was just a hunch. Maybe, the pursuit of old things didn't really affect Ron.

I decided to spend the night at the house on Pendrill Street. I was too tired to drive home, and it was late. There were the usual dogs howling and snarling between the pack outside. I'm not sure what they fed on or why they clawed at the door. My mind was busy. I needed to relax into a sleep.

In my dream I have the urge to dig. I scrape at the turf and bury my fingernails in the dirt. I rake at the small stones and gritty earth. I dig as a compulsion. It's heavy going at first, but I grit my teeth. There is something in this. I dig. I scrape away the soil with my hands until my fingers bleed and the salty sweat drips from my clammy chin. I dig. Soon, the earth is loose. It's easier now. It rakes away like it's been excavated before. There are growls. There are the whimpers of dogs fighting. I wake from my sleep disturbed.

What could it mean? Was it a metaphor for digging through my Grandfather's past? I wiped the sweat from my brow. I listened to the wind outside. The dogs were still foraging in the garden. It was still in the early hours of the morning. I brought a stale blanket from the airing cupboard and soon fell into a fitful dream again.

The dogs were snapping. They barked and howled as they fought amongst each other. Some of the animals had claw or bite marks still fresh with blood. Others had wounds that had dried and matted their fur to their wounds. I dug again. I had no need for a spade. I wanted that relationship with the dirt. A spade or other garden tool would have removed me from feeling at one with the dust. I wanted the immersion. I don't know why. It was just a really strong, lasting urge. I was digging like an animal. My clothes were covered in grime. It was almost like I was digging for my life.

I scraped and clawed and dug and raked. The earth was looser now, and the roots were sparse. I flung the mud away. The piles of detritus were mounting as I burrowed. Some of the dogs were at my heels as I scraped and clawed at the soil. I kept digging. There was a buried presence, I felt. There was something drawing me in. It was an intense magnetism. I was alive as I burrowed. I cleared the way with my paw-like hands.

I dug and scraped. I clawed the dirt. Then, I heard a low commotion underground. I dug, breathing and gasping, until the noises became louder. It was blacker than night. I kept clearing the way until I could discern vocal cords. At first, I thought the rasping was singular. It sounded oddly melodic yet deep like bass notes. I dug and cleared until the voices were separating into a harmonious choir of several people as they chanted. I couldn't see anything in the black of darkness. I kept scraping at the soil. My ears became keener as my eyes were blind and the smallest of sounds were magnified. Something was coming my way.

I heard a low scrabbling as something panted. It brushed by me. I could discern its nakedness as I was temporarily pinned against the wall. Whatever it was, it didn't put up a fight as it pressed past at chest height. It was running between four legs and two. First bipedal then on all fours –

as if undecided on which to adopt. It made its way towards the night sky. I steadied my breathing and pressed on to whatever pulled me to dig.

The voices were getting louder now. I kept burrowing down. My eyes were now well accustomed to having been underground for so long. There was a small light. I cleared the way towards the Earth's core. It was warmer than I might have imagined. The voices got louder. Some were low pitched. Some were much higher. I dug and cleared. I found joy in the clearing away of dirt. It became more natural and less of a chore. There was a rocky opening ahead. It was some kind of cavern. There were definitely dogs down here, I knew. I could hear their growls and whimpers. I kept clearing until I could stand upright. My back ached less than it should. I observed from behind a rock.

There was a marble altar with debris scattered on it. Several dogs sniffed and barked. Their growls reverberated. Other figures appeared to be human and they were muttering or chanting. It was damp as water dripped through the porous roof. I tried not to make too much noise. My heart pounded against my chest. The figure, around which others gathered, was not altogether human. His body was matted with dense hair. Those around him were in different stages of transmogrification. Some were more dog than human, and some were still able to use the vocal cords they were born with. My eyes widened. And then I nearly shrieked with horror.

I had to stifle my disgusted shock. How long had I been digging? It seemed like a few hours, but my observations suggested much longer. My fingers were encrusted in grime. Or what was left of my fingers - they'd strangely clumped together. My arms too, were more sinuous and covered in dark hair. I began to reel in terror. I wanted to crouch. It strained my back as I stood. One of the dogs sensed me. It bounded over towards where I hid and bore fangs as it snarled. I couldn't placate it.

"Show yourself," one of the figures ordered. I hesitated. And yet I didn't feel afraid. I felt... unsure.

I came into full view of those around the Altar. I brushed past several of the dog people. They smiled. They seemed to smile, anyway. Then my eyes widened in recognition. I saw who was at the head of the gathering. On his face was the familiar mole. I tried to mouth 'Grandad'. But my physiology no longer allowed me to speak that human word. I had become one of them. I realised that is why I was unafraid. And yet I still was able to vaguely question. Even though I couldn't ask.

My Grandfather was clumsier now. His paws were as mine, yet he was still able to coax his mole on his furred cheek. "Welcome to the pack," he laughed as he manipulated his growth. He didn't seem to be the man I knew. He had far less patience and my hackles raised. I looked at the monsters around me. I felt fear and dread. "Gather him," the man hounded.

42

I was grabbed by several of the followers. I wanted them to get their filthy paws off me. What were they doing? And then it dawned. I was to be the sacrifice. There was nothing I could do. A part of me wanted to fight. But I still possessed enough humanity to not want to go on as what I'd become. Maybe I could end this in the next life. I surrendered. I gave myself over to them completely. They led me to the sacrificial table. I happily lay down on my side as a dagger flashed. The last thing I remember is the metallic taste of blood as my earthly life essence drained. I prayed that, in death, I could become something bigger and end this travesty. I prayed until the light went out.

A Face at the Window

I can't remember what I was watching but the lights were low. I'd just settled down after chasing about after my daughter. She has to leave every light on in the house. It was more conducive for winding down now with just the small lamp on. I was beginning to nod off. But the soundtrack picked up on the box and I was paying attention again. Someone jumped out of the bushes. It was a cheap jump scare. I was getting bored as I looked for Tiger. She'd been among the scraps, on the plates, on the kitchen side and had knocked a spoon onto the floor earlier. It really winds me up when the cat is on the kitchen side. It's not very hygienic. A few weeks back we'd awoken to the smell of gas in the morning. Tiger had brushed against one of the knobs on the hob. I was livid. "That cat is a bloody health scare waiting to happen."

The cat is behaving strangely. "I think she's had a stroke," Patricia says. I disagree. She's probably just been fighting or is missing her mother. I get up off the sofa to have a look. A face presses against the window.

"Who the hell is that in the garden?" She saw him too. "I'll go and have a look," I say.

"Well, be careful," Patricia replies, pulling at my sleeve. I dash out of the back door as the fence is disturbed. He's jumped over it. I'm still in

44

my slippers as I slip out the back gate. The path is well lit with streetlamps. He runs past the gardens. I look behind me. My daughter has her arms crossed at our back gate. I'm not sure why I carry on. The man has definitely legged it.

Even Patricia had said it was a man. Now, I'm not so sure. There was something about that face that I can't put my finger on. It was weird but almost in a flash and I've a hunch that something wasn't right. I feel a bit uneasy as I carry on walking. I wish I could place why I feel that way. There's a clatter. I look through the open gate. Two men push me aside with their arms full. They're laughing. I'm aware I'm alone so I don't challenge them. I'm just compelled, like a moth to light, to look around the neighbouring garage. They've definitely ransacked it. I look around to see what's missing. But it's absurd. I don't know what was there in the first place. I don't want to be blamed. I don't want to explain myself if I get caught in the stranger's garden. Then I see a curious green bottle on the work bench by a lathe. I pick it up. I'm not sure why. It smokes and the face appears. His eyes are set too wide apart. I gasp. I flounder. He says, "I grant you three wishes."

I shake my head. "What? No. I just want to go home." It seems really foggy. I lose track of time. Then I'm sat on the sofa in my living room.

Patricia asks, "Are you alright, Dad?" I nod quite absent-mindedly. I can't really work it out. "I'm off to bed. Goodnight, Dad." She kisses me on the forehead. I look at the wall. What the hell is going on? After a time, I decide to retire. As I lay in bed there are shapes in the dark. I remember Patricia saying, "It's time you found a new lady friend." The double bed is definitely cold.

I drift and I wake. It's lonely at 3am. I slip my jeans and a t-shirt on. I slip downstairs for a smoke. I pass the curious bottle near the kettle. It is ornate with something like Arabic raised on green glass. I open the door to let my cigarette smoke out. I light my fag and a man dashes in. He's looking around. "What the fuck are you doing?" He's searching then pushes past me on his way out. I watch him, in shock, as he runs out the front gate. It slams shut and open in the wind. The bottle is still on the side. "I definitely need a woman," I mutter. The smoke rises in the cold early morning air. It's smoky as I remember those eyes set apart. Then I go blank.

The fog clears and I'm leaning on the cemetery wall. It's as light as day. I hear a disturbance by the gravestones and a beautiful woman walks towards me. She has dark hair and olive skin that's highlighted in moonlight. I decide that she is everything I could ask for. She is my every wish. "Actually, Michael," she reads, "you have one left. So make it good." I chuckle, looking into the depths of her green eyes. They are like a Mediterranean spring. They dance like the flashes of silvery fish. She is naked, and I'm enchanted as we embrace. We kiss.

My tongue probes her mouth. It brushes to know her. This exotic has secrets. She reciprocates. Her teeth sharpen and her skin falls away. I pull back to see a wasted Ghul. This djinn feeds on flesh to flesh herself. It is a shadow of the woman who knew my name. I stumble against tree roots. Her claws outstretch. Again, "I wish I was at home," I shriek. As she reaches to tear me apart, I fall back onto my bed. I scream. I'm filmed with sweat. My daughter's eyes adjust in the dark as she knocks and peers round my door.

"You've been wandering again, Dad. You're covered in mud." I tell her that I'm alright. She goes back to bed and I steady myself. I undress from my dirty clothes and uneasily lay down. The moon is penetrating the thin curtains. I hear Tiger downstairs, on the kitchen side. That spent green bottle definitely needs to go back.

We Are Beneath

I can't tell who she is in this dark, but it sounds like she needs urgent attention. It's dangerous to go above ground. They try to steal your face and your vitals. There's a market for internal organs. Those with money also want to thwart the facial recognition cameras that are peppered everywhere. "We need to get her to a doctor," someone shouts. "There's complications."

I have helped deliver a few babies over the years, but this one doesn't look good. Her stomach seems to be writhing or undulating or something. The kid must be made of strong stuff. He needs to be in this world. There's still law and order, on the streets, above ground, but it's limited to only protecting those with money. The rest of us have been sent to Hell. "A fucking doctor. Now!"

We make a makeshift stretcher with several jackets and ease the stranger onto it. Conversations are a rare commodity. "What's your name?"

I think. I can't remember. The name Callum comes to mind. "Cal," I say, "just call me Cal." He pats me on the shoulder in an unfriendly way.

"Grab that sleeve. We need to get her some help." We lift her up and stumble in the dark.

There are puddles everywhere. The limestone walls drip with rainwater. It's been like this, I guess, for perhaps two years. I'm guessing the year is 2046. Any notion of time has gone to pot though. We press on towards the pinprick of light. All I hear are feet splashing, water splashing, and this poor lady's anguished moans. I don't know the other three stretcher bearers. I stumbled across them as I looked for food. I just hope they pull their weight. We try to work as a team.

I left my fully furnished house about two years ago. It was comfortable but no longer affordable. Many people have deserted their homes. They've just thrown their arms in the air and said, "fuck it." It didn't help when Government surveillance started entering our homes. Everyone had to install cameras. Then people woke up to the notion of there not having been a public/private divide for years. The unaffordable home was now a prison. Unless you had a lot of money, you had to conform. But the populace didn't work together. They were too entrenched in the lives of celebrities and getting their 'me time.' When it was too late, it really was. Surveillance had gone too far. You couldn't fart without a Government Department monitoring it.

They said it was for our own safety. They blamed it on refugees and the millions who belonged nowhere. Thousands no longer have Citizenship. They just move from pillar to post like leaves blowing in the wind. We were playing computer games when they bombed a lot of countries. We needed 'me time.' The right-wing press pushed the 'dangers' of the other and Nationalism took hold. We didn't like foreigners.

People didn't talk much amongst themselves either. They were too busy with their technologies.

"We need to get a move on. She's struggling," one of the lead men ordered. There is more light now. Her stomach is undulating violently. The child is threatening to rip out like a whale breaking surface for air. We stumble and splash. I can see the exit now. We stop for a breather.

Those who could afford to eventually moved into gated communities because it was too risky on the streets. Then, they got too expensive for some. The super-rich left for a fortified Island in The Pacific as the rest of us were left to rot. They wrung the economy dry as best they could. Every last profitable drop was hoarded offshore. I'm hoping people will bounce back.

"She'll be getting cold on this damp floor. Come on." We resume our sleeves and press on. I can see the man beside me. He is really pale, almost skeletal, and squints as if the light is too much.

"She's not pregnant, you know. She's..."

The man in front pipes up, "Steve. I'm sick to death of your bullshit conspiracy theories. Shut the fuck up, for crying out loud." Steve mumbles something. I see he has no hair. Neither have the two men in front. I start to wonder what I must look like. The light is blinding as we exit above ground. "Lower her, a minute."

The man is unsteady on thin legs. He's cautious too. We wait as he looks for danger. Steve starts talking about a facility that isn't working on the remit in its mission statement. He's talking about social experiments but shuts up when the lead man returns from his quick reconnaissance. He's staring at the floor and shaking his head. It doesn't look reassuring. "Come on. We need to get her there. We'd better be quick." He looked to be almost naked. I think about mole-rats when I notice his top incisors.

We lift the expectant mother again. The light is dazzling. She's getting heavy now. I wish she would quieten down, but I try some empathy. There are old newspapers blowing against our shins. We wade through rubbish that is being looked through by others. They're scavenging for something to salvage and sell. I'm not sure what they'll do with the money though. It's almost useless. A lot of the shops are boarded up or have been ransacked. There's graffiti and not many windows intact. A woman is arguing with her reflection in a wine bottle. People have lost self-awareness. They're pacing and shadow boxing with their mirror images like animals in the zoo.

We tread carefully. A man, or what's left of him, is littering the path. His face is clean off. I can see the muscles and tendons where his lips were peeled away. There's a stiff grimace below the lifeless eyes. I shudder. I pull my jumper up over my mouth. The matted wool catches on my teeth. I didn't notice this change before. The air is noxious too. Again, I don't know why. The only cars I see are abandoned. The rusted remains are breaking down like prehistoric carcasses. People are wandering aimlessly. They're talking to heavy, thin air. I look up to the smog and hold my breath. Then I gasp. I'm exerting myself with this stranger.

We cross the empty road. There are empty houses left abandoned to rot. People didn't want the ties anymore. The expense and the surveillance made homes a costly prison hung around home-owner's necks. Bizarrely, I think, in amongst the rows of overgrown gardens, I see a woman painting her fence. I almost laugh as I feel something akin to hope. She is singing amongst the chaos in her own small bubble. She's different to us. She looks like how we used to look when we integrated above ground. I think the darkness has taken its toll. I feel self-conscious when she smiles and purses her lips. We're changing to suit our surroundings.

I know nothing about these three other stretcher bearers. All I know is Steve's name. They're ugly looking bastards too. The woman grabs my left wrist in agony. I'm pushing ahead with the other three. I see her belly contorting. That must be some baby. Then doubt sets in. My mind resembles the smog. I'm wondering why these men are helping this woman. What is there to gain from it?

"What about you, Steve?" He looks away, saying nothing. I ask the man up front. "Hey? What's your story?"

He exhales. "I'm Ron. I was a copper. My wife and daughter didn't trust me. They left. I was being policed more than I was policing. They grew tired of my questions and mistrustful too. I was part of the regime, I guess." I think that Ron is pretty open. He's less agitated than he came across when he was berating Steve. I choose to trust him. He is oddly open though. Maybe, I'm not used to conversations or personal disclosures. It seems strange given how much we're laid bare to the cameras.

"Thanks, Steve. Someone I can trust. At last," I say.

He laughs. "You can trust me."

I bat a strange insect from my face. The woman is reaching a torturing crescendo. "There'll be help shortly." I'm not sure she hears me.

There is silence. Then Steve talks. He's nervous. Almost apologetically nervous. "I was a Vicar, you know? I mean, before society started to break down."

I listen. "Is it the end times?"

Steve smiles through his teeth. "Well, no. I don't think so. Not yet. I mean, there's still hope. There is..."

Ron interrupts. He theatrically clears his throat for peace. Steve looks away again. We pass bodies strewn across the road and the path. The flies are busy amongst the litter. I'm about to talk to the other man in front but someone is shouting. A few youths come towards us. "We're not looking for trouble," growls Ron, straightening up to appear taller.

The teenagers are laughing and pulling faces. They're nibbling like rabbits to mock us. A knife flashes. "Have you got any spare innards? Maybe, we'll just take them."

Steve repeats himself. "I said..."

The boys laugh. "I heard what you said, Ratman. Now, scurry away before we carve your fucking tails off." He licks the serrated edge. We look ahead. They laugh as they disappear. We're nearly at the medical centre now.

The gangs have been busy. There's blood where the bodies lay. They're cut open and their organs have been pillaged. Some of the corpses have given up their faces. I wonder why the cameras never seem to see these mutilations. Maybe, they do. Perhaps there's just no-one to police the streets. That or no-one cares. We pass more victims. The others barely raise an eyebrow. Above ground, it's such a common sight now. It's hard to imagine anyone who lacks empathy.

I remember a debate at East Yorkshire University many moons ago. It's since closed down because people couldn't afford it whilst others didn't value education. It must have been difficult to teach the kids they live in a meritocracy before the primary schools closed down. During a seminar, we argued whether watching horror films would impact on viewers' behaviours. Many said it would. I guess it's a kind of 'you are what you eat' scenario. But that was years ago. People are desensitized now. Some even sell their own body parts because they don't trust their own organs. I'm surprised there are not more diseases about with all this bloodletting.

"You're a bit quiet," I rasp to the silent one in front.

He is pulled from his thoughts. "It pays to be quiet," he says. I feel a bit weary. He hardly seems approachable. Even if he is helping this woman.

"What's your name?" I ask again, with more compassion. He hears the humanity in my voice.

"I prefer not to say. I've seen and said enough. There's no harm in that, is there?" He is brusque.

"I guess not," I reply. "It's not like we're building trust or anything."

The silent one chuckles. "Once I've done my good deed, I'm fucking off," he says. "I agreed to help. It's not the same as marriage."

I am taken aback. "Suit yourself."

We approach the old medical facility. It's an ornate, grey-stoned Victorian building. There are bars covering the old windows. It looks like some sort of asylum. The gardens are well kept, and the exterior has been looked after. We push through the dark blue wooden doors. It smells of disinfectant and overcooked vegetables. It is unusually quiet. No-one is there to greet us. There are just the wails from down the corridor and a bit of commotion upstairs. We place the woman on a table. Steve is having an accident. There's urine splashing on the tiles.

"I can't...," he pleads, then takes flight out the entrance. He looked scared.

The silent one strokes her hair with his pale, bony fingers. His fingernails are grimy. "It's alright now, my love."

I laugh. "What? She's your wife?"

He looks up and nods. "Yes. That's right."

I am astonished. "You never said," I say.

"You never asked," he replied. I can't believe his lack of gratitude. I can't understand his guardedness. I am really uneasy. The woman is screaming in pain. Her stomach is writhing and she's gasping. She's almost having a fit. The disconnected telephone is knocked to the floor. Someone comes downstairs. Others, in white scrubs, walk up the corridor towards us. They grab Ron. He shouts out as they inject him. He flops as he's dragged subdued down the corridor. His feet drag as he's pulled.

I back towards the doors. The escape route is behind me. The silent one pleads for them to help his wife. She is foaming at the mouth. Her eyes are flickering. Then her stomach bursts open and flies pour out. The writhing must have been their larvae. "Fucking Bot Flies?" She settles down. She's dead. The silent one tries to scramble past. He's tormented at what's replaced his son. He's clawing the door. I can't escape.

I bolt past as they inject him. I run down the corridor. There are odd smells. I run past the ward where people are screaming. I run to a large set of heavy white doors and push my way inside. The smell is formaldehyde. It's a sickly smell combined with what it's preserving. They're doing bloody experiments. I see in a mirrored medical cabinet. I too have shed hair. My milky eyes lack pupils and my teeth protrude over my bottom lip. I am much more gaunt and grey than I was. My dull, inexpressive eyes well up. They are lifeless. I cry tears.

Around the lab are clear vats and bodies encased in glass. They look more animal than human. There are people like me and others like elephants. These specimens have been tampered with. They're in various states of amputation. These bastards are treating us like monkeys and rats. I hear people hurry. They look in. They stand and search. I let out a gasp as the heavy door slams behind them. I regulate my breathing as I hold my chest steady. I need to get out. I count to...whatever. Then I break for it.

I run and run and I don't look back. I don't think about the experiments and I don't trip over the bodies on the path. I don't react to the lads who wolf-whistle and threaten to carve my heart out. I don't think about all that. I just hobble as best as my crooked, bowed legs will let me. I don't know what to do or who I can trust. I can barely trust myself. I really can't trust my own image. I look like a bloody rodent. I run and I dodge. I gasp and I run. The world is starting to spin as I run straight into the arms of a woman. She drops her paintbrush and scratches behind my ear. I might feel relieved much later.

The Interwoven

No-one hears the trees scream as they burn. Even the firefighters can't put their fingers on the shrill screams of anguish. It is proving fruitless to arrest the fires. Local people blame the blaze on arson. They no longer listen to the mounting evidence around global warming. The politicians have been playing it down for too long and the public have lost faith in the police. Too many people have been going missing and nothing is being done about it.

Simon Broadbent recognises this. He knows it is easy to commit a murder. His brother has been sleeping with his wife. Michael had been confiding in Emma because of the stress of firefighting. They don't know that Simon saw them. He's managed to keep a lid on his anger since he stumbled across them cavorting in his bed. Emma doesn't know why he's behaving differently towards her. She has been uneasy. Wanting to please her husband more which Simon finds repulsive. He will deal with her later. He smooths his field jacket, wraps a scarf around his nose and loads his van up with flammables.

Simon isn't great with expressing his emotions. He mistakes the anger in his chest as a heart problem. He will get this checked out once he's finished with the cheating bitch at home. How could they? His own brother too. The back-stabbing bastards, all loved up with their legs wrapped around each other. It was difficult, in the half-light, to know whose arms belonged to whom as they made their baser instincts known to one another in his bed. Well, tonight they are going to pay with the ultimate sacrifice. He fights back the warm tears on his flushed face.

He pulls up along the muddied track. Simon can see the fire engines a way ahead. He needs to be quick. He quietly shuts the van door as noises travel further at night. Then he grabs the Jerry can out of the boot and slams it. *Shit! I need to be more careful*, he thinks. The trees are unusually quiet for the amount of company that the fire vehicles suggest. There were four crews at least. But Simon has yet to see any fires. He pulls his scarf up and heads into the darkness.

It is still. Not even the birds are calling, and the moon is wrapped in clouds. The heavy Jerry can bangs against his knee. He thinks he sees a few trees moving. He pauses to listen. Simon can feel his heart against his chest. *Please don't have a heart attack now*, he almost pleads. *At least let me torch the bastard first*. There is nothing but the lull of leaves and his breaths. He tries to regulate his breathing as he heads further into the trees.

Then there is the rhythmic chanting. It is imperceptible at first. But the sounds of human vocals can't be mistaken for anything more bestial. Simon draws nearer. He can't believe his eyes. He rests against a tree trunk as his night vision adjusts. *What the hell are they doing?* The gathering is definitely a crowd of firefighters. They're wearing their protective clothing and chanting in the clearing. Simon is taken back to his glimpse through his bedroom door. He is trying to displace himself. He sees his wife and brother interwoven as they passionately fuck. Simon grits his teeth, squeezing his eyelids together in pain.

He is back in the trees. The chanting is strangely melodic. Is it a sacrifice? Are they praying to someone or something? It's hard to tell from where he is watching. The fire folk are waving their arms in the air and looking up to the sky. A light flashes. Simon pulls back. He doesn't want to be seen. The illumination picks Michael and his crew out. Simon is furious. He bends to unscrew the Jerry can and pours the fuel out amongst the detritus and bark. "I'll burn these bastards."

The chanting reaches a crescendo. Simon strikes a match. Then he feels extreme pain. A twig has pierced beneath his fingernail. It burrows. He feels the bloodied fingernail peel off. Another gorges into his ear and something woody wraps around his leg. There are different sounds. A whisper perhaps – like the wind in the trees. A vine wraps around his throat and tightens. Simon starts to panic. He tries to break free. But it's fast becoming a losing battle. More wood spears his orifices or makes new bloodied entries. His stomach is enmeshed with the trees.

Then he sees them. A wooded gnarly figure peeling away from the trunk. It leaves an indentation where it'd hid. There's another. The congregation cheers. They throw themselves to the floor. The Sons of Bark creep towards the new captive. Simon screams out as his eyes are pierced with branches. His nerves are on fire. They scream to remain human. He is becoming stiffer. The ground has claimed more blood. Simon's sight fades as his hearing becomes more pronounced.

The staked remains of Simon gurgles its final plea. The crowd runs to where he is being pulled into the canopy. Michael notices the spilt fuel canister. "Burn the bastards," he screams. He searches for his lighter. His colleagues feel displaced. One of the men throws up as a wooded figure takes his throat with a rough hold. More of the bark figures descend on the men.

Michael fumbles for his lighter, but something rakes against his ear. It scrapes, "You too belong to the wood. The trees are branching out." Michael doesn't know whether to laugh or cry. He gasps and flicks the flint. But the trees work their way into his flesh. They rip and tear and puncture and writhe until flesh becomes dead vegetation. This is how nature will fight back against deforestation. For nature always finds a way. It finds a woody way to Michael's heart and strangles it in its grip until it beats no more. That is the lay of this land.

Scare the Crows

"Are you sure this is the place?" Fish pulls his drenched collar snug to his chin. He shivers and looks around with narrow eyes and his mouth bubbles with rain. The manure smells fresh on the open fields. There is diesel on the wind that gusts through the courtyard where the farm machinery rusts against the neglected cowshed. Everything stinks of shit. The rains have been relentless.

"It's only for the night," replies Tom. "We can walk to Hellerington by mid-afternoon, tomorrow." He sounds as flat as the East Yorkshire fields. He turns to Fish. They both hesitate. "I'll knock," he says. Tom doesn't like the look of the farm. He thinks it looks desolate. Fish bangs on the door again.

A hunched woman in a shawl answers. She can't look up with her spine curvature. She whistles through false teeth. "You can sleep in the barn," she points with a gnarled finger, clutching her shawl. Her eyes are milky. They don't meet theirs.

"She's hiding something," whispers Tom as the elderly owner goes inside. They notice her standing back at the window. The men trudge through the puddles and the muck. The barn, opposite the shed, is just as dilapidated. The roof lets in water. They drop their rucksacks and slump down onto the hay bales. The night is drawing in. "Is there anything to eat?" Tom rummages through his kit for some snacks. "Fuck's sake. I'm starving. Them biscuits won't even touch the sides." Fish fills his mouth with a whole custard cream. It tastes good. Tom dances. He pops outside to relieve himself. The loud rain snaps on his orange cagoule. Fish waits inside. He taps his feet. Tom's been gone a while.

Fish checks his watch again. Someone flashes past the chink in the door. It looked like a naked child. Fish gets up to check it out. He wonders where the hell Tom is. The low, thick clouds make the dark feel closer. The albino is disappearing into the tall crop. There's no sign of his friend. Fish follows the boy into the head-height harvest. The stalks are wet yet brittle. He rakes through, sweeping his arms wide. It is deathly quiet. He sees Tom's discarded jacket hanging from the barley. Someone is behind him. Fish stops and crouches down. Someone is pushing through the same path. It's the old woman.

"I'll help find your friend," she whistles.

Fish mutters, "How do you know he's gone?"

The woman grins as best she can. "They all go," she replies, "those that stay. Why else would you be here?" Fish thinks he's glad he's not alone. The woman doesn't reassure him though. They sweep through the crop in the heavy dark. There are noises; shrilled clicking and commotion as the field is disturbed. Fish slows but the hag pushes him on to a clearing. The clearing is disturbed.

Fish sees that the pale boy isn't a boy at all. Though it's the height of a ten-year-old. It is pale, skinny and naked with the others. Their eyes are black. Their mouths are wide with needle-like teeth in wide grimaces too big for their amphibious faces. They're clicking to each other as they lurch on webbed feet. Fish sees Tom. Parts of Tom. He wants to scream but retches instead. Tom's lifeless eyes are stuffed with the harvest. His mouth and ears too. His head has been hacked from his body. They look like sick taxidermy. Fish wants to run. But the woman is strong with her children.

The toad folk click. Fish can't see. The pale things are swimming through his tears. He can't scream. Images of scarecrows dance through his head. He wonders if they'll eat him.

The gelatinous webbed hands remove his coat. Fish tries to kick. The weight of death is upon him. He screams. He screams and he pleads as they remove his coat and boots. Then there's the scratching. Brittle stalks are pushed into his ears. His nerve endings scream like pricked heat as the crop pushes deeper. He screams, "No. Please, no." But Fish is being stuffed. His mouth is dry with barley and they penetrate his eyes. Everywhere. His whole body is flashing pains as stalks jab nerves. He relieves himself. Fish has forgotten the severed Tom to his own struggle. They don't hold back.

Anywhere he can be violated the pale amphibious things stuff. He feels full and surrenders a laugh as he thinks of a Christmas turkey. Then

65

they carve. They hack to make new body holes for the barley. Fish can taste blood. His exposed leg amputation feels the cold against nerve heat until he passes out. He floats as the field diminishes. Then he is elsewhere.

The cavernous cave is throne to the urchin King. That royal pond-life slumps on a barnacle encrusted seat of power. Its many eyes search the dark as it looks on its toad minions. They're dancing everywhere. They are still, like rock, then flash in dance. The lamp fires lick the cave as the shadows beat too. Fish will not be eaten. At least, not today. He is part of the trawl. All around he sees others. His dismembered head looks upon something that was his leg. It is quite apart from him now. It's something else to see his hacked part, standing quite alone, as it scurries on spidery legs through the cold rock. The barley has imbued the body bits with a new dark life.

Each dismemberment is in its own bloody element. These parts are the whole new harvest reaped from bloodied fields. The aquatic King garbles orders. His subjects subject. They pass through the rock back to the fields. They dance. They click and they dance until a new reaping stumbles upon them. They dance as they lurch in fields to stuff the stuff of nightmares.

Charity Bins

I don't know much about the virus. I just need some milk. It's late and I'm not keen on popping to the shop at this hour. At least the nights aren't so dark. It's still warm at 10.30pm. I close the door behind me. There's the neighbour's rubbish strewn across my lawn. They never get their bins out on time. I cross the road and realise I've forgotten something. The bathroom window is still open. I shouldn't be gone long.

The back of the shops is awful at night. There's usually someone going through the industrial waste bins looking for anything the charity shop has slung out. Sometimes, people drink there or inject where it's quiet. There's always crap everywhere once people have rooted through the cast offs. I usually cross over. Even though I don't have to. I manage to avoid any encounters doing this. It smells of rot.

I cross onto the other path. It's poorly lit in those shadows behind the shops. I see shapes. The hairs on my nape stand up as a shiver makes me shudder. They're just strange. I can't work them out. I pass, quickening my step. Then, I cross back and get some milk from the convenience store. Heading back, I can hear them rummaging through the bins. Those strange shapes, behind the shops, on the other side of the road. I hurry home to make a brew. As I unlock my front door, I feel really uneasy. But I can't say why. It's just a hunch. The stench of fish hits me as I lock the door behind me.

The rancid stink reminds me of a virus that's been in the news. It's world-wide. The virus has been altering people's appearance and behaviours. I try not to feel negative. But I can't locate the smell. It's like that around the charity shop bins. I don't know. I put the milk on the kitchen side. I flick the kettle on. A noise. A bang from the bathroom. I freeze. Someone is shuffling in my bathroom. There are people in my bedroom too. *What the hell?* I listen. Then I pick the biggest knife up. My palms are sweaty. The kettle is too loud.

Whoever the noisy bastards are, they're quite light on their feet. It sounds more like the scratching of large rats. I take a deep breath. I charge through to the bathroom. There's no point holding back. There's a strange shape over the bath. I stab. I stab and I stab and I stab like someone who has had their personal space violated. There are shrieks of death throes from the strange shape. My hands are sticky. I'm about to flick the light on when I'm clawed.

I try to struggle. There's the stench of rot. The light through the open window picks their pinched features out. They've got narrow eyes and whiskers. I'm seeing things. But the rat people pin me down as I drop the bloodied knife. They're upon me. More man than rodent, the virus is turning them into vermin. They scurry about. They have strength in numbers. I'm bundled up to the loft space in the roof. The rat people bind me with electrical cables.

I'm gagged. No-one will know I am here. My mother hasn't phoned in months.

I try to break free. It's the first time I've sat still in ages. The rat people are everywhere. They've taken over my flat. As my mind works overtime to think about escape, I notice something strange about myself. The electric cable cuts into my wrist as I gasp in horror. I am one of them.

The Darker Side

She hasn't phoned me in three days. I can't understand it. She always phones. Saying that, these last three days have been really fuzzy. The nurse said I was found wandering the streets. I was bundled into an ambulance by the police and I'm being washed out with antibiotics. Meningitis is a strange gig. I wouldn't wish it on anyone.

I came 'round to find myself on Ward 18 in a hospital bed. I'm not keen on hospitals. Too many people. I'm not, what you might call, a people person. Especially if they're sick or dead. I was keen for a coffee and a ham sandwich though. I hadn't eaten for two days. The police had said I'd been a right handful. I'd even lashed out at a few nurses. I really wasn't quite myself. Apparently, I'd reverted back to being a four-year-old. When my Mam phoned, I was calling her 'Mummy' and I couldn't even remember Dad. At least I have an excuse; the virus had altered my behaviour temporarily. I just don't know where Kate is. It's strange.

"Mr. Keith Jefferson?" I look up at the nurse in anticipation. "You can go home now. Just collect your discharge papers at the reception desk." I thank her. I try to phone Kate again to no avail. The phone just rings. I pack my bag and collect the documents. At least the buses are every ten minutes. I sit near the back, downstairs on the red double decker.

Passengers are on their phones and children are messing about.

"I know it's hard. But don't you find that a birth usually follows a death?" The young woman nods into her mobile. I found that when my brother passed away. His wife was due and gave birth two weeks later. I think there's a pattern to everything. A cause and effect. When someone passes on, a new life takes their space on this planet. I wonder why Kate hasn't phoned. She's really supportive usually. I find my front door open.

The living room looks like it's been burgled. The television screen is cracked. The set lays upended on the carpet. Furniture is strewn everywhere. I panic. "Kate? KATE?" I search the kitchen and bathroom. I dash upstairs. "Kate?" The bedroom. She must be there.

Her legs are on the bed. Her head is twisted on the floor. "Oh my God!" I mutter. Kate has angry bruising around her throat. She's been dead for days and the window has been closed. I ease her body back onto the bed. I hug her and sob. Who the hell would strangle her? She's never upset anyone. I should phone the police. I should phone them straight away. But I can't leave Kate. I can't. Her eyes are so child-like in death. I cuddle her and sob. I run my fingers through her blonde hair and press my forehead to her cold, grey face.

I can't leave her. I can't. Then the noises start. Her dressing table is upturned. "What the fuck?" I shout. "Who's there? Who is it?" There is no-one. There's no-one but an angry energy throwing cushions and clothes and Kate's stool at me. I dodge the airborne furniture. There's so much vehemence. "Kate? KATE? Is that you?" A bedroom cabinet is pushed over. I reel. My head swims. Kate's lifeless body is looking somewhere I can't see.

I curl up. My chest is tight. One of her favourite shoes bounces off her dressing table mirror. As the lipstick scrawls on the glass, she really doesn't need to spell out the awful truth.

The Miskatonic Madness

"What is that author called? The one who wrote about The Old Ones. He wrote *Dagon*." The University librarian's brow furrowed as it clouded over outside. He glanced out the window at the darkening sky. The weight of sleepless nights was carried in his face.

He leaned over. "Sir! That author is H.P. Lovecraft. And you must act fast." I leaned back and appraised the stark terror in his eyes. He was bordering on madness. It was as if something from another dimension was colouring his frenzied mind. As the clouds gather, this soul stands testament that Cthulhu will return.

Burnt Offerings

The meal tasted bad the first time. I taste the burnt pork again as I grip the wicker cage. I should not have come here to The Village with no signposts. No wonder no-one knew the way or its ways. I know my fate as I appeal to my one God.

The heathen chant for their panopoly. My clothes are singed with the flames. The acrid smoke pricks my nostrils. I am to be offered like their missing children. I implore them to rise above their base intellects. But they know better. I will burn for their ripe, fruitful harvest.

Gravestone Anguish

You can hear her anguish from the dark Attic window if you pass the cemetery at night. She screams like an animal. I can hear her hooves on the wooden floor. She paces, lashing out at the locked door. Imelda no longer recognises me with those demonic eyes. I long to return my simian wife to her former self. The lover before I dabbled.

Slouch at night against the cold stone of the dead and you'll hear something melt your marrow. Her goatish gait paces until the darkest hour when she will break free and I shall conjure no more.

Hackles

I can scarcely read the scrawl as a bony claw falls heavy on my shoulder. The unknown breath smells of rotting fish. Its grip tightens as I stumble with the invocation. The words are ancient, and the dark is getting darker. My mouth is dry. I feel terror rising in my chest.

If I don't read, the ancient scaly thing will impale me on its talons. If I carry on, I will give rise to other monstrosities – perhaps even more persuasive and terrible. I pause. That hairy nuzzle presses into the back of my neck. I feel my hackles rise.

Sons of Bark

The moon filters through branches to the unlit forest floor. The leaves seethe, brushing against my ankles. The trees mutter that I'm lost. I try to retrace my steps to find the muddy path. I stumble. There are pains as I face the midnight clouds.

They are part of the bark. Those ancient ones peel away from the old tree trunks with their gnarly forms. They leave imprints in the trees where they hide. Their twig hands descend upon me to make the woods that little bit more expansive. I scramble to evade the trees. They take what was me.

Surrogate Corpse

She is always replacing things. Just as I get comfortable with a sofa it's gone. I can never relax at home. She can't tell me why she feels the need to do it. I think she is between hobbies. "One day, you'll replace me," I tell Vanessa, half-joking. She really puts me on edge as she never talks things through. I am never part of her decision-making processes.

We can't have children. I wonder if this accounts for her refurbishing our home all the time. Maybe, Vanessa just doesn't like cleaning. I don't know. I came home from work and my favourite coffee table was gone. I was so used to putting my tea there. I get angry and tight-chested. I just can't get through to her. I dread working at the shipyard for fear of what I'll come home to. She really fucks me off. I make it known too.

I phone Vanessa after lunch and apologise. I tell her I'll be home late as it's busy. There is a freighter in that needs work. The early evening is lost to welding the hull. I think about the phone call afterwards. She'd been really absent.

I am glad to get home. It is quiet and the living room light is off. There's some chicken curry in the microwave. Vanessa must be feeling under the weather. I warm my meal and eat it alone. I kick my shoes off then pop upstairs. She is asleep. I quietly undress and slip in next to her. It smells of fish and there are tiny movements. The sheet feels like the rice I've just eaten. I flick the light on. There are fucking maggots everywhere. I pull the duvet back and throw up. Vanessa has been busy. My ex-wife hasn't weathered well. She is almost rotted beyond recognition. There is a note: 'You're next.'

I wonder where Vanessa is. She's never been this unhinged. She could be hiding anywhere with a spade or a hammer. I thought I really knew her. I am naked and vulnerable. I slip a dressing gown on and quietly tread to the bathroom. My heart feels like a ticking bomb. I gasp. She's not there. I turn to the spare room. The curtains are drawn. I peer into the darkness. I can just make out shapes in the dark, but I don't recognise some of them. Then I jump. The lock turns behind me.

Deep End

Me and Ralph have dived a lot. We've never got in any scrapes, touch wood. Today, we're off the coast of Mexico. It's sweltering. Ralph is really animated. He expects to see some new species of crustaceans. We don our wetsuits and breathing apparatus. I go first.

It's really unusual. I want to tell Ralph to 'hang fire' but he's already catching up. The water shouldn't be this dark yet. We're not deep enough and the sun is in the sky. I put my head torch on. Ralph tugs at my leg. He has noticed the lack of light too. We decide to go on. There should be a cave below where archaeologists have been exploring. We swim deeper as a shoal of bright fish pass by. It's definitely dense. The sunlight is barely illuminating the shallow corals.

Ralph points to the cave entrance. It looks chalky. He gives me the thumbs up. I swim into the gloomy mouth where several eels appear. They are feeding off some dead mammal or fish, I imagine. Ralph is close behind. My torch penetrates the rock. The cave seems vast and volcanic. I press on. There are starfish and species of silvery bottom feeders that I can't identify. Ralph tugs my leg. He tugs it again, more urgently. But it's not Ralph.

I see a watery shadow in the depths. I wonder where Ralph is. The figure is a woman with long, loose hair. She draws nearer as I panic. She is horribly deformed. There are craters on her skull which reminds me of syphilis. And she has been struck by hard blows several times. It looks as though the hammer had been embedded. She is almost skeletal. I think that the eels stripped her flesh in her sleep. I try to give her a wide berth.

I'm against the rocks. She has no eyes. I stare into the abyss of the dark sockets. Her maw is agape with a few teeth. She raises her hand, covered in barnacles, and pulls the snorkel from my mouth. She hooks her fingers. I gag as she pulls at my tongue. I need air. I'm taking in water. Then I see Ralph.

He is already bloated. He is caught then breaks free. His body floats upwards. The last thing I see is his wide, cold face. Then this relic woman squeezes me free of air and I succumb to the depths.

Artist @A_Welchman

Acknowledgements

'The Prairie Lures' (c) 2019 by Mark Anthony Smith, originally published in *The A-Z of Horror: A is for Aliens* by Red Cape Publishing.

'Wood Fooks' (c) 2020 by Mark Anthony Smith, originally published in *The A-Z of Horror: B is for Beasts* by Red Cape Publishing.

'The Clifftop Terrors' (c) 2020 by Mark Anthony Smith, originally published in *The A-Z of Horror: C is for Cannibals* by Red Cape Publishing.

'What the Trees Recall' (c) 2019 by Mark Anthony Smith, originally published in *The A-Z of Horror: D is for Demons* by Red Cape Publishing.

'Keep It Inside' (c) 2020 by Mark Anthony Smith is unique to this collection.

'Crown of Slugs' (c) 2020 by Mark Anthony Smith is unique to this collection.

'The Call to Dust' (c) 2019 by Mark Anthony Smith is unique to this collection.

'A Face at the Window' (c) 2020 by Mark Anthony Smith, originally published in *The A – Z of Horror: G is for Genies*.

'We Are Beneath' (c) 2020 by Mark Anthony Smith is unique to this collection.

'The Interwoven' (c) 2020 by Mark Anthony Smith is unique to this collection.

Also from Red Cape Publishing

Anthologies:

Elements of Horror Book One: Earth
Elements of Horror Book Two: Air
Elements of Horror Book Three: Fire
Elements of Horror Book Four: Water
A is for Aliens: A to Z of Horror Book One
B is for Beasts: A to Z of Horror Book Two
C is for Cannibals: A to Z of Horror Book Three
D is for Demons: A to Z of Horror Book Four
E is for Exorcism: A to Z of Horror Book Five

Short Story Collections:

Embrace the Darkness by P.J. Blakey-Novis
Tunnels by P.J. Blakey-Novis
The Artist by P.J. Blakey-Novis
Karma by P.J. Blakey-Novis
The Place Between Worlds by P.J. Blakey-Novis
Short Horror Stories by P.J. Blakey-Novis

Novelettes:

The Ivory Tower by Antoinette Corvo

Novellas:

Four by P.J. Blakey-Novis
Three by P.J. Blakey-Novis
Dirges in the Dark by Antoinette Corvo

Novels:

Madman Across the Water by Caroline Angel
The Broken Doll by P.J. Blakey-Novis
The Broken Doll: Shattered Pieces by P.J. Blakey-Novis
The Vegas Rift by David F. Gray

Follow Red Cape Publishing

www.redcapepublishing.com
www.facebook.com/redcapepublishing
www.twitter.com/redcapepublish
www.instagram.com/redcapepublishing
www.pinterest.co.uk/redcapepublishing
www.patreon.com/redcapepublishing

Printed in Great Britain
by Amazon

55038120R00050